HUGH PINE

and the Good Place

HUGH PINE

and the Good Place

Janwillem van de Wetering

Illustrated by Lynn Munsinger

Houghton Mifflin Company Boston   1986

Library of Congress Cataloging-in-Publication Data

Van de Wetering, Janwillem, 1931–
  Hugh Pine and the good place.

  Summary: Hugh Pine, a porcupine, decides to live
alone on an island in order to get away from all the
problems the forest animals bring to him; but after a
time he decides being alone isn't so wonderful after all.
  [1. Porcupines — Fiction. 2. Friendship — Fiction]
I. Munsinger, Lynn, ill. II. Title.
PZ7.V2852Hv 1986   [Fic]   86-3108
ISBN 0-395-40147-X

Text Copyright © 1986 by Janwillem van de Wetering
Illustrations Copyright © 1986 by Lynn Munsinger

Printed in the United States of America

V 10 9 8 7 6 5 4 3 2 1

HUGH PINE

and the Good Place

Chapter 1

IN THE NORTH of this country, all the way to the east, you'll find the county of Rotworth. From its fields and hills you can see Sorry Bay and the little island in the middle. The sun rises from behind the hills and dips way into the bay, and all the mornings and the evenings have a deep red glow.

Rotworth itself is just a little town with a few weathered buildings. The most important building is the post office, which is owned by Mr. McTosh. Mr. McTosh is five foot small; he wears white whiskers, and when he isn't behind his counter selling stamps, he also wears a long coat and a red floppy hat. What Mr. McTosh likes to do most of all is hike in the woods and the fields or take his boat out on Sorry Bay.

On the highest field, which slopes down toward a cove that is part of the bay, stands a tall pine tree all by itself. On the tree's highest branch lives Mr. McTosh's best friend. His name is Hugh Pine, and he

1

also wears whiskers and a hat and a coat. What Hugh Pine likes to do most of all is look down on the beautiful countryside, and beyond, to the bay and its island. Once in a while he climbs down and wanders about, ripping a bit of fresh bark from a tree, eating some crisp poplar leaves or munching on berries or nice, tasty mushrooms. When Hugh goes to town, after walking up the long winding Sorry Road, he visits his friend Mr. McTosh.

Hugh Pine is almost four foot small and that includes his hat. That's really quite tall, for Hugh is a porcupine, the biggest and cleverest of his tribe. He's so clever that he can even speak a little Human. On the road he walks upright so that he won't be run down by cars. When the drivers see him they think Hugh is a little old man. Most of the time they wave to him, and Hugh always waves back. Mr. McTosh and Hugh look remarkably alike, and a lot of people think they are brothers.

Hugh is usually happy when it's not too hot. When the sun has been burning down on his tree all day, Hugh gets a little bothered. Then he climbs down, puffing with the heat.

One day Hugh was looking at the bay below, at the

long cool waves. He thought about how nice it would
be to change into a water animal once in a while.
Water animals are never hot.

Puffing and huffing, Hugh ambled down to the cove.
Smooth white rocks line the muddy beach down there.
Hugh climbed up on one of them and sat staring at
the water, which was pushed closer and closer by the
incoming tide. He wondered whether he could swim.
As he sat and thought, the water was suddenly all
around the rock. Hugh knew about the tides. After a
while the bay would pull back again, and he didn't
mind waiting. He looked at baby herrings, glinting in
the sun, dancing up and down, this way and that, all
at the same moment as if they were listening to slow,

lovely music. Above him eagles soared, dipping or raising their wings, following smooth circles. The baby herrings were cool below the water, and the huge eagles were cool above. Hugh still felt hot. He took off his coat and hat, but he couldn't take off his thick hairs and all his quills, the long sharp spikes that all porcupines wear. Quills can be handy at times, for they keep away big bothersome beasts that jump at you and bark and snap their jaws, but on a hot day they tend to be a bother.

A seal came by, darting along with the strong current, splashing with his flippers and blowing bubbles from his nose.

"Hi," said the seal.

"Hello," Hugh said.

"Coming in?" asked the seal.

"Do you think I could?" asked Hugh.

"Easy," the seal said, slithering up onto the next rock. "Here, I'll show you." The seal dived in, disappearing in a series of foamy circles. His head came up again. "See?" The seal had business farther along in the bay. He shot off, turning through the water, waving his flippers.

"Hmm," Hugh said. He had taught himself how to walk upright, but he remembered how silly he had looked when he kept falling over and had to pick himself up. Teaching himself to swim might be a foolish exercise, too. He'd rather not be seen. When you try something new, other animals always think you're funny.

Hugh felt the water. Yes, it was certainly nice and cool.

Now, would he try or would he not?

He could see himself swimming gracefully like the seal, being an acrobat afloat.

There then. *SPLASH!*

Hugh went under, but only for a second. He popped up, carried by the air caught in his hairs and quills. He rowed his strong legs and waddled his short spiky tail. Hugh snorted happily. This was easier than he'd thought. Out and away! Perhaps he could reach the quiet little island.

As he swam out, the tide pushed him back, and he didn't seem to be getting anywhere. A big wave washed his hat and coat off the rock, and he had to catch them on his nose before they could sink and be lost forever. Hugh grunted and snorted, paddling back to the beach.

What was that noise?

He pushed the hat from his nose with one dripping paw and tried to shake the coat away so that it wouldn't block his ears. There it was again, that same nasty noise.

Hugh peered from under his tufted eyebrows, which had gotten soaked and were flopping down.

There they were! Two red squirrels, hanging from their little hands, holding on to a branch. They were laughing at him! And some stupid rabbit was giggling under a bush.

"Go away!" Hugh roared.

The squirrels and the rabbit ran off when Hugh dragged his clothes ashore. He snarled at them, baring his big orange teeth. "Botherers," Hugh grumped. "Always around when you don't need them. Tittering and grinning. Forever in the way!"

"Bah," Hugh grumbled as he climbed back onto his tree.

He sighed when he had reached the highest branch, resting his squat body on his strong, short tail. It was still far too hot, and the breeze was dying down. He looked unhappily at the bay. Down there the cool wind blew strongly, and the island sparkled like a jewel between the foam caps of the waves. The island was a little hill, lined with a golden beach. On the hill grew a pine, just like Hugh's tree, waving its graceful branches.

That's the Good Place, Hugh thought. It'll be much nicer out in the bay.

But how could he ever get there if the tide kept pushing him back?

Hugh dozed off sadly. "The Good Place," he muttered. Then he dreamed. He was in the Good Place, surrounded by splendid solitude. How marvelous the Good Place was.

Chapter 2

"Sir?" a squeaky little voice kept asking.

The sharp little sound had nothing to do with Hugh. Hugh was asleep. He had dreamed himself away from the heat and the bother. He wasn't around. Hugh had dreamed himself free.

"Sir?"

Hugh's paws began to flutter.

"Sir?"

Hugh's tail began to tremble.

"Sir?"

"BRRAH!" Hugh roared.

"It's me, sir," the red squirrel shouted, hopping away to the end of the branch. "Me, sir. There's some trouble."

Hugh shook his prickly head, trying to get back his dream, which had broken into a thousand brittle pieces.

"Now what?" Hugh snorted. "What trouble? What

has your trouble got to do with me? Why can't you let me sleep? Don't you know this is my tree?"

"Yes, sir," the squirrel squeaked. "Sorry, sir." The squirrel tripped over his own tail and fell off the branch, but managed to grab hold just in time to hoist himself up. "Big trouble, sir. Those gray fellows are all over the place again and won't listen to us. Big gray fellows, sir. They're such unmannered louts."

"Gray squirrels?" Hugh asked.

"Yes, sir, and everybody knows that these woods are Red Squirrels Only. They just have to leave."

"You wouldn't be," Hugh said slowly, "that nasty little chap who was laughing at me when I took a dip just now."

"Me, sir? Never."

"Why don't you go away?" Hugh asked.

"And the gray squirrels, sir?"

Hugh stared. The red squirrel waited.

"Oh, very well," Hugh said grumpily. "Fetch the biggest gray squirrel you can find. Bring him here. Take your time. You should know by now that I hate all hurry."

The squirrel rushed off.

"If I don't take care of this," Hugh said as he tried to get comfortable again, "they'll be all over me all day. Whirring and chattering. Shouting and going *yek-yek-yek*. Can't have that. Bah! Bother!"

The squirrel came tearing back, making a red streak through the tree. Just behind him was a gray streak.

"Sir?" the two squirrels squeaked.

"Back already?" Hugh asked. "I thought I asked you to take your time? Now what *is* this trouble?"

"It's *him*," the gray squirrel said. "Him and the other little red fellers. Throwing nuts at us, sir. Won't leave us alone. Yelling. Being a nuisance."

"Now," Hugh said heavily, "you're new here, I believe. Do you know who I am?" As he spoke his quills rose slowly and his large orange teeth shone.

"Yesh," the gray squirrel said, holding on to his mouth, to stop it from trembling. "You take care of trouble, shir."

11

"I don't like trouble," Hugh said as his quills stood straight up, making him bigger and bristlier than ever. "You wouldn't be thinking of *making* trouble?"

"No shir," the gray squirrel squeaked.

"Very well, then." Hugh pointed. "See that poplar at the end of the field? The gray tree with the little round leaves that are always moving?"

"Yesh." The gray squirrel nodded.

"That's the line," Hugh said. "You fellows stay on the left side and you —" he glared at the red squirrel "— you stay on the right. Is that clear?"

"Left?" the gray squirrel asked, looking at his paws, holding up one and then the other.

"Right?" the red squirrel asked, also looking at his paws. He waved one. "This side, sir?"

"That's the *other* right paw," Hugh said. "No. I mean, that's not right."

"These ones?" the gray squirrel asked, waving both his paws.

"Never mind," Hugh said. "Look. See the way I'm pointing? That's your side. Okay? And that side is for the others. Got that clear now?"

"Yes," both the squirrels said.

Hugh Pine rattled his quills. "And, mind you, I'll be watching. And mind another thing, stay away from

this tree. No mistakes. No noise now. All of you leave this pine alone."

"Thank you." The squirrels tumbled away.

"Sillies," Hugh grumbled. "They'll never remember. And while they forget there'll be noise all over."

The quills settled on his back as he gazed at the bay. The tree on the island was beckoning him. "The Good Place," Hugh whispered. "How will I ever get there?"

Chapter 3

"SHUFFLE, SHUFFLE, SHUFFLE." Hugh Pine snored softly.

"Turrrrr, urrrussssh." Hugh's strong jaws smacked a few times, then veered open in a big sleepy yawn.

"HELLO?" something shouted from below.

Hugh's mouth snapped shut. His eyes snapped open. Something wrong somewhere again. He peered down. Below, in the bushes, twigs cracked, branches shook, and dry berries clacked against each other. "HELLO?" something kept shouting.

There are all sorts of noises. There is noise-noise that maybe will go away if you leave it alone, and there's calling-noise that gets worse if you don't do something about it. This appeared to be calling-noise. It always hits you at awkward times, like now.

"WHAT?" Hugh Pine shouted.

"HELLO? HELLO? HELLO?"

Hugh saw a brown rabbit running about on the pine

14

needles below the tree. The rabbit suddenly sat still, twitching his nose, waving his long ears. "Lost my hole, sir," the rabbit screamed. "Can't find it anywhere. Please come down and help me find it."

Hugh began to climb down. He knew all about rabbits. Rabbits never give up once they have some nonsense started. Rabbits are full of grief that always requires immediate attention. Rabbits get wronged a lot and have to be righted right away.

"Holes don't run away," Hugh said as he plopped on the ground. "Tell you what you do. Hop about a bit until you fall in it."

"But I've done that, sir," the rabbit whined. "Now my feet are all sore and my tail got hooked on thorns and the squirrels keep laughing at me and . . ." The rabbit was crying.

"BRRAHH!" Hugh roared. "Stop your whimpering, you rascal. I know who you are. You were giggling at me when I was swimming in the cove."

The rabbit wriggled away.

"Silly!" Hugh rumbled. "Tell me more about your hole."

"Oh, it's beautiful," the rabbit cried. "There's an elderberry bush growing all around it, and inside there's a corridor that leads to a hall, and there are rooms on all sides, big ones for parties, and little ones for snoozing." The rabbit got even more excited. "I plan to have a family, you see. There's this other rabbit I met, only half the size of me, and she has this itsybitsy tail, and floppy ears and all, and she's waiting for me to finish the hole —"

"Yes," Hugh said gruffly. "So there'll be lots of you soon, tumbling over each other, making messes that I can sort out for you, I bet."

"But where's my hole?" the rabbit cried.

Hugh stared at the rabbit. "Rabbit," Hugh said slowly, "I'm sorry to tell you that your hole is gone." He held up a paw. "Don't be sad now, rabbit. You can make an even better hole. I know just the place, about a mile from here. Follow me and I'll show you where to start digging."

The rabbit began to sniffle. "It's close, sir. It took

me such a lot of effort, carrying all that dirt away, all that planning and working, slaving and drudging. How could it get lost? *Please* help me find it."

"Elderberry bush, eh?" Hugh asked. "Big bush or small bush? Tall bush? Fat bush?"

"A round bush," the rabbit cried.

Hugh walked ahead of the rabbit. There were quite a few elderberry bushes about. Soon it would be time to harvest their fruit. Did he really have to share a good crop of berries with a family of fluffy sillies?

The rabbit sobbed behind him. "My hole! My hole!"

The hole was probably close, for rabbits, once they're settled, do not like to stray. The rabbit whimpered even more loudly. "I'll never have a hole. I'll freeze. I'll starve."

Hugh stuck his tail into the soft ground, pushing it in firmly so that he could sit at ease. "Now, rabbit, good luck comes to those who keep trying. What are we looking for? For a hole in a bush?"

The rabbit ran about, lifting branches, sniffing under the grass. "So well planned, sir, running water and all."

"Close to the brook? But the brook is over there!" Hugh said gruffly.

Together they followed the water rushing over polished stones, lapping at little banks covered with fresh moss.

"There," Hugh said. "That's a round bush."

The rabbit cheered.

"You can thank me now," Hugh said sternly.

"Thank you!" the rabbit shouted and fell straight into his hole. "Thank *youououou* . . ." His little voice disappeared into the ground.

Hugh shrugged. He walked back to his tree and mumbled furiously while he climbed the trunk. He was tired and it was still hot.

Chapter 4

NYEE! NYEE!

Ten thousand mosquitoes rose in a solid black ball, dancing up to Hugh's branch. They were hunting their last meal of the day, after having rested above a nearby pool through the afternoon heat. Their scouts, ripping free from the ball, buzzed about Hugh, smelling his blood. They whipped back and reported. The ball fell apart and all the mosquitoes zoomed in. Hugh tried to swat them off, but they were coming from all sides, gliding down his quills, digging about under his hair. Hugh slid down the tree, turned a somersault on the needles below, and humped away as fast as his short legs would carry him. He aimed for his final refuge, a hole that he dug many years before and had almost forgotten. It was a big, dark hole between the roots of an oak. Hugh didn't particularly like burying himself deep under the earth, but it's good to have a safe hiding place in case . . . well, just in case.

Hugh tumbled into the hole.

"Hello," said a welcoming little voice.

There wasn't much light so Hugh had to wait until his eyes got used to the dark. Who would dare to sneak into his very own hole? The hole that had cost him such a lot of trouble? He still remembered the heavy rocks that he had rolled back to the light.

It was a baby fox, curled up in a nest of dry weeds.

"You live here?" Hugh asked.

"I was born here," the little fox said, wobbling his pointed ears and sweeping the weeds with his little bushy tail. "Who are you?"

"This is my hole," Hugh said, looking about to be sure.

"I think it's ours," the little fox said. "My parents say nobody is supposed to come here but us. What a strange animal you are! What are those long things that stick out of your back?" He tumbled about Hugh. "Would you like to play?"

21

Hugh folded his quills down so the little fox
wouldn't get hurt. "Not really," he said.

The mosquitoes whined outside. Hugh had been too
quick for them, and they didn't know where he had
gone.

The little fox showed off his toys, a yellow plastic
bottle and a paper cup and some string that he had
found.

"Very nice," Hugh said. Would those nasty bugs be
hanging about forever?

"Do you have any toys? Will you bring some when

22

you come again?" the little fox asked, waving his bushy tail.

Hugh pushed the paper cup about, to keep the fox quiet. Finally it became quiet outside, too.

"Would you like to see my pinecone collection?" the little fox asked.

"Later," Hugh said. "Must go now. Good-bye."

Hugh dragged himself back to the pine. It took forever until he could settle on his branch. The moon had come up and painted the bay silver. The island glistened.

"Ohhh," Hugh Pine groaned.

Chapter 5

HUGH WAS UP early the next morning. It was going to be a hot day again. While he looked for breakfast the squirrels whirred about, wanting him to explain again which side was what. The rabbit showed up and introduced his fiancée, and the baby fox wanted to know if Hugh had time to look at his pinecone collection now.

"Not today," Hugh kept saying.

A committee of three porcupines waylaid him near the shore. "Hugh," the littlest porcupine said, "there'll be a meeting soon, and we want you to come."

"Be sure to be there," the other two porcupines said. "You missed a few meetings, and your absence has been noted."

"Yes," Hugh said crossly. He thought meetings were a waste of time.

The three porcupines ran after Hugh. "Where are you going?"

"Swimming," Hugh said.

"Porcupines don't swim," the biggest of the three porcupines said.

"They don't walk upright, either." Hugh turned around, bristling his spikes. "And they never wear hats or coats. You know what porcupines do a lot? They bother their betters."

The two bigger porcupines sniffed and left. The littlest porcupine smiled. "Oh, Hugh!"

She sat on a rock while Hugh took off his clothes. "You never told me you could swim."

"I can," Hugh said, "and I'm swimming away right now." He pointed to the island. "That's the Good Place out there. I'm going to live there forever."

Her soft voice sounded lonely. "Don't you like it here, Hugh?"

"Too noisy," Hugh said, sticking his legs into a wave. "Everybody is always up and about. Won't leave me alone. Even my tree isn't safe anymore."

"Please stay," the littlest porcupine said.

"No," Hugh said and splashed down, sending up a curtain of drops. "Come in," Hugh shouted. "It's easy."

"Oh, Hugh," the littlest porcupine cried. "Must you really be so strange? You know I can't swim. Nobody I know can swim."

"I can," Hugh said and paddled away, caught in the tide that drew him out. "Bye now. Do take care."

Hugh drifted farther away, at ease on his back, splashing with his tail. He looked over his shoulder, but the island was still far away. He turned over and pushed his legs as hard as he could, but the turning tide pushed him back again.

The wind strengthened and the waves broke over his head. The shore came closer.

Hugh felt very small, a mere speck in miles and miles of tumbling water.

Better get out of here, Hugh thought.

Then he was out, stuck in a mud bank, with rocks around, covered in slimy weeds. He slithered about.

Something loud roared and barked between big boulders.

"Hello," Hugh said.

A seal struggled weakly in a bright yellow net. It was the seal who had showed Hugh how to swim. The seal was struggling to get out of the net.

"What happened?"

"Don't rightly know," the seal said. "I was frolicking in the waves, having a good time, and then I got caught in this thing. Help me, will you? There's a good chap."

Hugh gnawed on the thick twine. "It's too strong," the seal said. "I've been doing that, too. I'll be in this forever." He twisted his sleek body and began to yap with desperation.

"I'll be back," Hugh said.

"Botheration," Hugh grumbled as he humped along the shore, looking for his coat and hat. "How come everybody is always in trouble?"

He found his clothes, put them on, and humped uphill to the Sorry Road. What's the good, he thought, of being clever here? It's trouble to get all those botherers out of trouble.

The tarmac of the road was hot and burned his feet, but finally he saw Rotworth lying ahead.

"Hi, Hugh," the people on the sidewalk said. They knew he was the little old man who lived somewhere in the Sorry Woods.

"Hi," Hugh said, shuffling along, walking as straight as he could and hiding his face under the wide rim of his hat. He liked the idea that people thought he was human, too.

The post office was busy, and he had to stand in line. Mr. McTosh was licking stamps. "Yes, what can I do for you?"

"It's me," Hugh said.

"So it is." Mr. McTosh walked around the counter. "Good to see you, Hugh. I'm just locking up. I brought in some pie today, must have known you were coming, and I've some iced coffee, too, and let me see, yes, here, my last old boot."

Hugh ate the pie, guzzled the coffee, and chomped away on the boot.

"Feel better now?" Mr. McTosh asked as Hugh was cleaning his whiskers.

"Yes," Hugh said. "Thank you. But there's some trouble." He told Mr. McTosh about the seal.

"Oh my," Mr. McTosh said. "And we keep telling the fishermen to be careful with their old nets. We'd better get going, Hugh. You can point the way."

Mr. McTosh got his car, and Hugh scrambled onto the front seat. The car went fast, and Hugh had to hold on to the dashboard. At the marina, Mr. McTosh held out his hand for Hugh to grab while he got down into the boat. They were both very careful because of the barbs at the end of Hugh's quills.

"Here we go," Mr. McTosh said, untying the rope that hitched them to the dock.

Hugh sat in the bow and got quite excited as the engine caught and a white wave sprang up, slashing past the boat's sides and bubbling up in a wide wake behind.

"A bit choppy," Mr. McTosh shouted. "Hold on now. Up and away!"

Out in the bay, a fin, taller than a man, sliced through the waves.

"A killer whale!" Mr. McTosh shouted. The whale

came up for a moment and looked at Hugh with a puzzled eye before disappearing. The enormous animal was more than twice the size of Mr. McTosh's boat.

"Where's this seal?" Mr. McTosh asked.

"Over there." Hugh pointed to the shore. The boat turned sharply, and Mr. McTosh shut off his engine and rowed toward the land.

The seal was no longer struggling but lay exhausted, with his nose pointing through the net.

"I'll have you out in a jiffy," Mr. McTosh said. "Just let me cut that nasty nylon."

Mr. McTosh's sharp knife cut easily through the twine, and Hugh pulled the net open. The seal pushed himself out with his flippers. He yapped happily before waddling into the bay. Mr. McTosh and Hugh watched him swim away.

"Are killer whales dangerous?" Hugh asked.

"They seem friendly enough," Mr. McTosh said, lighting his pipe. "But then, I've always been in my boat. They do have lots of teeth. I'm not sure what they would do if they met us when we were swimming."

"Mr. McTosh?"

"Yes, Hugh?"

"Do you see the island there?"

Mr. McTosh looked. "Surely, Hugh. I sometimes stop there when I go fishing."

"Does anyone live there?"

Mr. McTosh scratched his whiskers. "No. It's rather small, you know. Just the hill with the pine tree and some bushes below. Nobody out there, rather a lonely place, I would say."

"Mr. McTosh?"

"Yes, Hugh."

"Would you take me there?"

"Just for a look?" asked Mr. McTosh.

"I'd like to live there."

"*Live* there?" Mr. McTosh asked. "But, Hugh, you'd be all alone. There's plenty to eat, but you won't have any company."

"That's nice," Hugh said firmly. "Could you take me there now?"

Chapter 6

THE ENGINE PLOPPERED while Hugh sat on a rock, ready to say good-bye. It was nice and cool on the island, and Hugh was all spread out, with his coat unbuttoned so that his pink wrinkled belly could catch the sun.

"Have to go now," Mr. McTosh said. "Sure you want to stay? I won't be back for a while."

"Sure," Hugh said.

"I'll have a bit of a holiday after the weekend," Mr. McTosh said. "Will be going away. Quite a bit of time'll pass before I can find my way out here again."

"Time," Hugh said dreamily.

Mr. McTosh laughed. "Time is a human thing, Hugh. You're better off without it. We people made it up, and now we have to run so that it won't slip away." He puffed on his pipe. "You may be stuck here though, I would think."

"Don't mind," Hugh said. "This is the Good Place."

34

He looked up at the pine tree on the hill. It was much
taller than his tree ashore. It was quiet on the island,
and he could hear only the sound of the waves. "Very
nice," Hugh said.

"Good-bye, Hugh."

The engine roared and the boat jumped away. Mr.
McTosh waved. Soon he was far away, and Hugh
walked up the hill and began to climb the great pine.
"*Yahoo*," Hugh shouted when he finally reached the
top. Alone at last. No one would ever bother him
again.

He licked the trunk's bark. It was salty from the
sea's air. He breathed deeply as he settled with his
feet curved around a twig. No rabbits. No foxes. No
bugs. No heat. None of the bothers.

Hugh yawned and stretched. What a lucky animal

35

he was. No porcupine had ever had such a magnificent island to himself. Here he could finally sit and think, dream, forget, become part of all the things he was not. Here, Hugh thought, I can be the sea, I can be the sky.

He drifted off into his first undisturbed nap.

When he woke he could hardly believe his eyes. The bay stretched on all sides, dainty clouds drifted high around him, calm waves caressed the beach below.

Beneath him the bushes' leaves whispered and a fragrance of fresh berries drifted up. Something to eat maybe, now, or a little later.

Hugh dined on ripe blackberries and licked some good strong salt off the rocks. He nibbled on a juicy root and went for a brisk walk to see all that was his own. On the beach lay a large shell. He blew into its open end, and a soft eerie sound filled the clear air around him.

Once he had walked around the island all his worries were gone. He could see that nobody else lived on the island. No one would bore him with worrisome tales. Alone at last.

"I'll be alone forever," Hugh promised himself.

Chapter 7

So THE DAYS and the nights passed. Climbing up and down the great pine provided good exercise, and when he had climbed enough, Hugh splashed about between the rocks. The juicy leaves of the bushes tasted good with the ripe berries. Nothing disturbed Hugh's pleasant long naps. Swinging on his favorite branch, Hugh grinned when he thought of what the squirrels might be doing, chattering and yukking, or giving out those sharp little cries that had always gotten on his nerves so much. The rabbit, no doubt, would have managed to lose his hole again.

And the littlest porcupine?

If that porcupine would only be just a little adventurous, she could be here with him, on the same branch, enjoying the splendid view. She sometimes did that in the other tree back there. Not too often, of course, for she knew that Hugh liked to be alone as a rule, but once in a while . . .

Hugh shook his head. No nonsense now. Why would he think of her? She was one of *them,* the busybodies who couldn't leave well enough alone. Always some trouble with the tribe.

No tribal trouble here.

No trouble at all.

He could just sit and think.

Mr. McTosh wouldn't be coming either, for he was on a holiday, whatever that was.

Hugh would rather be on his branch, swaying, dreaming.

Hugh thought of the pies that Mr. McTosh often carried in his satchel. A big slice of Boston cream pie, a grand helping of pecan pie, a large piece of black-berry pie.

Well, Hugh had blackberries here, more than he could ever eat.

He wouldn't mind a piece of boot, though. Soaked in strong coffee.

That afternoon, out for his walk, Hugh found a boot on the beach. It was the biggest boot he had ever seen. He tore it to pieces and chomped away. Nice strong taste. Tastiest boot he'd ever eaten. Or was it?

Usually while Hugh ate a boot Mr. McTosh sat next to him, puffing on his short pipe, telling a tale. It might be about fishing on the ice, or about the time he saw

a white shark, or about what he had done to shoo away the bear who had been at his honey.

It was strange that there were no birds.

Hugh occasionally saw a seagull planing over the waves at a distance, or eagles drawing rings high above. Back home there had always been birds about — loudmouthed jays with their brilliant blue feathers, tumbling about the pine; chickadees buzzing and chirping to themselves; and the bright yellow grosbeaks, descending suddenly in a great flock. Noisy, nasty birds. They couldn't make it this far to his island.

No birds.

Nice and quiet.

Hugh dozed off and dreamed about the baby fox. Together they romped on the beach and found a ball.

The little fox gamboled about, pushing the ball, re-
trieving it from the surf, bouncing it off the soles of
his feet. Hugh and the baby fox were laughing a lot
together.

"This is the Good Place," Hugh told the fox.

"Indeed it is," the baby fox said. "How clever of
you to find it."

The baby fox was right, but he wasn't around when
Hugh woke up.

Hugh climbed down and circled the beach, taking
long strides and keeping his head high. "My island,"
he said loudly. "The Good Place. All mine."

How beautiful it was. Above him the bushes carried
their loads of fresh fruit. Fish played between the
boulders that rose from the pools. Hugh splashed in.

"Hi, fish." The long silver shapes darted away, afraid
that the prickly animal would grab them.

"Can't talk to dumb fish," Hugh told himself.

What had happened to the seal? Surely the seal could come to the island and bring some friends, and they could all sit around and talk for a while.

Maybe the seal could take him back. It was too far to swim, and somewhere in the bay the killer whale lurked, the giant dark shape with all the sharp teeth.

Not that Hugh wanted to go back, but it would be nice to know that if one day, some day far in the future, if he wanted to travel, for a little while, maybe the seal could give him a ride.

Back on his branch, Hugh saw the seal. Its body rose up, a long way out. Down the seal went, up he came again.

"Hey! Hey!"

Hugh almost fell down the trunk. He rushed to the beach and scrambled onto a rock. "HEY!"

No seal.

Seals don't look at land much. They have no business on land. Seals live in the sea.

Well, there was plenty to eat, and Hugh liked it all. Berries. Roots. Poplar leaves. No complaints.

Nice and quiet.

Just the sounds of the sea.

Such beautiful sounds.

Hugh sighed and sat on the rock, waiting.

Chapter 8

IT WAS SATURDAY, and Mr. McTosh closed the post
office after a busy morning. He wondered what he
would do that afternoon. It would be nice to sit in his
garden a while and look at the flowers or watch the
hummingbirds standing still in the air, sucking nectar
from delicate blossoms, their wings moving so fast
they became a blur.

"No," Mr. McTosh said. "I must really chop some
wood."

After lunch he fetched his ax. *Whop*. The log split and
so did the ax's handle. He was about to throw it into
the woodpile when he thought of Hugh Pine. Hugh
always liked chomping on an old ax handle. He would
give it to Hugh when he went out Sorry-way again.

Then he remembered. Hugh now lived on the island.
Hugh wanted to be alone. "In the Good Place," Mr.

McTosh mumbled. He wondered how Hugh was making out on the bay.

Mr. McTosh's little house and beautiful garden were a good place, too, miles from the traffic and busyness of Rotworth.

He strung up a hammock between two trees and lay down for his nap, wearing only his long johns and his hat. Now he was just as happy as Hugh on the island.

Mr. McTosh smiled in his sleep, but in the middle of a snore he shivered and woke up. He had dreamed about Hugh, and Hugh was *not* happy. Hugh sat on a rock and stared at the sea, waiting. Waiting for what?

It was just a dream, of course.

Mr. McTosh tried to get back to sleep. What did he know about porcupines, anyway? Maybe Hugh needed to be alone for a while, just like Mr. McTosh himself. Mr. McTosh looked at his driveway. He was alone, but people were always welcome to visit.

Should he go and visit Hugh? He didn't want to bother his good friend. There Hugh was, enjoying his lovely surroundings in perfect peace, and there Mr. McTosh would pop up, pushed by a noisy engine in a boat banging on the waves.

"Sleep," Mr. McTosh said firmly.

The hammock wasn't so comfortable anymore. A fly buzzed by. It was pretty hot in the garden. Maybe he should go inside.

"Hugh is my friend," Mr. McTosh said as he swung his legs out of the hammock. "That means we must be alike. I wouldn't like to be stuck on an island. For a day, maybe. After that I would be lonely. I'm going to see Hugh, whether he likes it or not."

Chapter 9

HUGH WAS STILL on his rock. He had been there all night, trembling, at times, in the cool air. Then the sun came up, and Hugh climbed halfway up the hill to eat a few berries, but they didn't taste very good. A thorn hurt his paw, and he went to bathe it in the bay. Then he scrambled back on his rock.

"I'm not waiting," Hugh said. "I'm just sitting here, taking in the fine view."

The seals swam far away. Their heads were black points on the water. Hugh didn't shout at them anymore. They didn't care. Nobody cared. "That's good," Hugh said. "All this caring is a lot of bother. I'm fine here, I don't need busybodies inquiring after my health at all."

He wondered what he should do. Sit in his tree? What for? Walk around the beach? He had done that so many times already his footprints covered the sand. It looked as though a hundred porcupines lived on

the island, but their prints were all the same. A hundred Hugh Pines with nothing much to do except feed themselves, but he wasn't too hungry.

The sun stood high in the sky and was beginning to come down. Another day half gone, another night to follow.

Hugh waited.

And then he heard something, *Plop, plop, plop.*

Hugh jumped up and took off his hat so that he could see better.

BRRRRRMMMM.

A noisy engine. Nice noise.

A fisherman going by? Passing the island at a fair distance?

No, the noise was coming closer.

Hugh slid off his rock and humped to the water's edge. He thought he recognized the noise. Could it be? Couldn't it just perhaps be? By chance, so to speak?

It was! *It was!*

Hugh jumped on a boulder and waved his hat. "Here! HERE!"

Somebody waved back. Hugh peered, shading his eyes with his paw. No! Or yes! That hat looked familiar. Hugh also recognized the boat.

"HEY! HEY!"

The boat came closer. Mr. McTosh looked a little strange.

"How are you, Hugh? Do you mind if I visit? How're you doing?" Mr. McTosh asked once he had pushed the boat onto the beach. "What's with you? Have you forgotten how to speak?"

Hugh was smiling too much.

He climbed aboard as fast as he could and sat in the bow.

"Don't you want to show me the Good Place, Hugh?"

"No," Hugh croaked. There was something in his throat.

"You want to come along? Isn't there anything you need to take? You've been living here so long, you must have some possessions."

"Just a minute." Hugh climbed out, ran to pick up the seashell he kept between two roots, and came back carrying it in his paws.

"Where do you want to go?" Mr. McTosh asked.

Hugh pointed at the land.

"Yes," Mr. McTosh said, "that's your old tree, all right. It looks kind of strange without you sitting near the top."

Mr. McTosh pushed the boat free with his paddle and started up the engine. The boat turned smartly as

he opened the throttle. It cut through a big wave, leaving a big foamy V behind. Hugh's quills were flattened by the wind. His big orange teeth glinted as he kept on grinning.

Chapter 10

"Afternoon, sir," the red squirrel squeaked, hanging from a branch. "Would you mind speaking to the gray squirrels again?"

"Sure," Hugh said. "No trouble, I hope?"

"Just a little," the squirrel said. "You see that spruce, sir? We're not too sure whether it's on their side or ours."

"You can share that tree," Hugh said. "Meet each other and share the news of the day."

"Thank you, sir. That would be nice."

"Hello," the baby fox said. "Where have you been? My parents have gone for the day, and I'm all alone. Would you like to see my pinecone collection now?"

"Of course," Hugh said, following the little fox into his hole. "What nice cones you have there. Shall I help you to find some more? Under my tree are some big cones. Let's go and pick some in the shade."

53

"Right," the baby fox shouted. "And afterward, will you teach me how to climb your tree?"

"Yes," Hugh said smiling, "and if you have time tomorrow, I'll teach you how to swim too; we can go to the cove."

"Wow!" the little fox shouted.

Later, it was evening already, and the rabbit came with his fiancée.

"I heard you found our hole for us," she said. "Such a nice hole. Thank you very much."

"No trouble," Hugh said. "Let me know when you lose it again for I will always remember where it is."

The Porcupine Committee came by, too. "We have a problem, Hugh. Your presence tonight will be appreciated by all of us."

Hugh was interested. "What's the problem?"

"Mushrooms," the biggest porcupines said. "There's a new type of mushroom growing in the woods. We're sort of wondering whether we can eat it."

"Maybe you can come and check," the littlest porcupine said. "You're so clever, Hugh, and we would just love to taste it."

"It's a risk, you see," the in-between porcupine explained. "Remember what happened when some of

54

the fellows tried the red-and-white speckled mush-room last year?"

"Some of us got very sick," Hugh said.

"Did you say *us?*" the littlest porcupine asked. "You always say *you.*"

"Like, '*You* fellows are pretty stupid,'" the biggest porcupine said.

"*Us,*" Hugh said. "I'm a porcupine, too."

The Committee left after Hugh promised to come to the meeting that night.

Chapter 11

ALL THE PORCUPINES from the Sorry Woods were sitting around the glade, waiting for the full moon. The soft white light got stronger and stronger, and then the moon appeared, gliding majestically over the tops of the tall trees. It hung above them like a giant silver disk, bathing the moss below with a splendor of silvery rays.

"Heee," the porcupines sighed, closing their eyes for just a moment. So quiet it was. This was indeed the place of dreams, the way it had always been, since ever so long ago, when the porcupines first began to gather in the glade.

When they opened their eyes again a dark shape appeared soundlessly from the woods, walking softly on the moss until it stood still in the middle of a round open spot.

"Hello," Hugh said. His voice was deeper and more melodious than the porcupines remembered.

Hugh lifted his shell and blew a long deep note that hung in the glade, filling the silence slowly, increasing in volume until all the forest listened.

"*TOOHOOOOO,*" blew Hugh.

"*AAAAHHHH,*" sang all the porcupines. They knew what to do. Up they were, standing on their hind legs as they rattled their long quills. "*RIC TIC TIC,*" the quills sounded briskly. Higher sounds were added, for the porcupines were shaking the spikes on their tails. They came forward and bounced back again, reaching out to each other with their paws.

"*TAHA,*" blew Hugh.

"*RIC TIC TIC tattle.*"

The porcupines danced while Hugh kept blowing on his shell. It sounded brighter and fuller now than it ever had on the island. He tapped his foot on the moss as the porcupines shook and shuffled, stepped this side and that, without ever losing a beat.

The dance lasted quite a while, until Hugh dropped his shell and the porcupines sat down on the moss, smiling happily at each other.

Hugh waited a bit for the mood to change. "Now," he said kindly, "what's this about the mushrooms?"

The Committee brought him a few. The mushrooms were small and yellow and looked juicy, with fat stems and thick round caps.

"You've never seen these before?" Hugh asked.

"Never, Hugh," all the porcupines shouted.

"That's true," Hugh said. "You haven't been around that long, you're too young, maybe you don't remember. So many of them used to grow here. Am I glad they are back."

"Can we eat them, Hugh?"

Hugh smiled. "But of course!"

The porcupines scratched their bellies. The red mushrooms speckled with white had looked good and tasty, too, but those who tried them had almost died of pain.

Hugh put out his paw. The littlest porcupine gave him the biggest mushroom.

"Thank you," Hugh said. *CHOMP*. It was gone. "I'll have the others, too," Hugh said, reaching out. *Chomp chomp chomp.*

All the porcupines watched Hugh. Hugh grinned at them. "Can I have some more?"

"Hurray!" the porcupines shouted and ran off to pick as many as they could. Only the littlest porcupine stayed with Hugh.

"Hugh?"

"Yes, dear?"

She touched his paw. "You blew on your seashell so beautifully, Hugh."

"Yes," Hugh said. "Sounded good, don't you think? I practiced a bit in the Good Place, but I never knew that the sound could be better."

"Let's go and eat some of those nice mushrooms, Hugh." She led the way to a moss field full of them, which she had discovered herself, but hadn't had time to tell the others about.

Chapter 12

"THERE," MR. McTosh said. "Hugh! How good that you could find the time to come by."

Hugh put a big brown paper bag on the counter. "I brought you a present."

"Something to eat?" Mr. McTosh asked. "Did you bake a pie?"

Hugh laughed. "Take a look."

Mr. McTosh peeped into the bag. "Hugh," he whispered, "that's my favorite mushroom. Very rare nowadays. And such a lot of them, too. Are they really for me?"

"For you, Mr. McTosh. I'm glad you like them."

"*Like* them?" Mr. McTosh shouted. "I *love* them. You've no idea how I've been longing for these. Come to dinner, Hugh, and I'll whip up a stew. With herbs and pepper and a pinch of salt."

"Well?" Mr. McTosh asked, ladling more mushrooms into Hugh's bowl. "What do you say? Isn't my stew great?"

"Very nice. Could you pass me the salt?"

Hugh emptied the shaker and grunted happily as he ate. With the salt, the mushrooms were even better. It seemed to bring out their subtle taste.

"Ha," Mr. McTosh said, "a feast for two kings. Anything else you care for, Hugh?"

Hugh rubbed his belly. There might still be a little room.

"Let's see now," Mr. McTosh said. "I'm out of boots right now so there I can't oblige. Ha! Wait a minute. I knew there was something else."

He brought in the broken ax handle. "A special treat I saved!"

"Thank you," Hugh said. His teeth sliced through the wood. Mr. McTosh looked on with admiration. He wished he had teeth like that.

After the meal Mr. McTosh lay in his hammock, and Hugh sat on his tail in the grass below. "You know," Mr. McTosh said, "I used to look for the Good Place, too. I was restless then and traveled all over."

"Did you find it?" asked Hugh.

Mr. McTosh made himself more comfortable in his hammock. "Sure," he said slowly, watching two beautiful butterflies doing an aerial dance just above his tum. "Don't you think it's nice here?"

"The Good Place is *here*?" Hugh asked.

"Wherever," Mr. McTosh said. He yawned. "But where's Where, eh, Hugh? Maybe Where is Here . . ." Mr. McTosh was falling asleep.

"Where," Hugh mumbled and held up his left paw. "Here." He held up his right. Then he put both paws together. Then he thought for a bit. Hugh's head began to nod as he listened to Mr. McTosh's gentle snoring. Hugh, sitting comfortably on his strong, solid tail, dozed off too. He was back on the island, but he wasn't alone. The red and gray squirrels gamboled happily in the pine tree on the hill, the rabbits cheered and chased each other on the beach, and the little fox arranged his shell collection under an elderberry bush. Mr. McTosh leaned against a sun-baked rock and puffed on his pipe. "Where you happen to be, Hugh," he said kindly, "the Good Place is too."